The Charm of the Defeated:

A Collection of Southern Short Stories

In loving memory of my southern mama,

Susan Ann

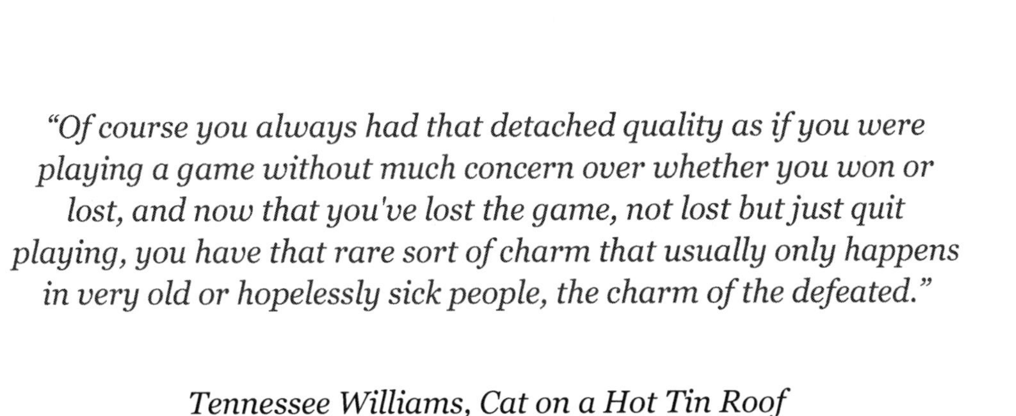

"Of course you always had that detached quality as if you were playing a game without much concern over whether you won or lost, and now that you've lost the game, not lost but just quit playing, you have that rare sort of charm that usually only happens in very old or hopelessly sick people, the charm of the defeated."

Tennessee Williams, Cat on a Hot Tin Roof

AUNT CORA LEE, 1988

In all the time I'd known my Aunt Cora Lee, she was on the verge of death. It crept upon her as she searched through the oak cabinets in her kitchen. She'd slam the cupboard doors on their old iron hinges, and she'd mumble softly at the pain in her chest, the burning in her lungs.

She would slowly shuffle to me sitting at her small kitchen table, and her weak and trembling hands would place a slice of zucchini bread before me on a daisy-covered plate.

"I had a hard time making this batch," she would say as she struggled to pull the heavy chair from the table where she'd sit down to rest and heave a collected sigh of relief.

"What's the matter today, Aunt Cora Lee?" I chewed the warm bread and studied the lines that covered her pale face. Rouge rested peacefully between the wrinkles on her cheeks.

"I just can't shake this chest pain. Doctor Ellis says it is heartburn. This ain't heartburn. This is a coronary waiting to happen. That's what this is," she grasped the heavy glass of iced tea and pressed it to her thin lips.

My grandmother said that Aunt Cora Lee had been dying for nearly sixty years. Ever since she was a young girl, she'd been plagued with some sort of ailment. She'd never been in the hospital for so much as a sniffle, but she was determined that she was dying. She was going Home to meet her mama any day now, for the last six decades.

My mama and daddy liked taking trips in the summer. They'd drive down to Biloxi and stay for a week and stop at every antique store and boutique and fruit stand on the way back home. There are a lot of armoires and fancy dresses and peaches between Biloxi and Itta Bena, Mississippi. That's why they left me with my grandmother for two weeks in June.

I liked staying at Granny's house. She had a big place on the north side of town. It was a lot of yard to mow and chores to do, but I didn't mind helping her. I liked sitting with her on the front porch swing to watch the deer, and I liked playing Rook in her kitchen with her best friends on Friday nights. Granny let me drink as much Coca-Cola as I wanted, and I got to stay up late.

My grandmother volunteered at the nursing home three days a week. Most of her friends were in the home, and she enjoyed reading to them, doing jigsaw puzzles and reminiscing about the old days at the Elmore Schoolhouse.

I didn't so much like going to the nursing home with Granny, though. It smelled like a baby's diaper, and I couldn't understand what old people said when they talked to me. So she left me with Aunt Cora Lee on those days. Aunt Cora Lee was old, too, but she didn't smell like pee, and I could understand most of what she said.

I always asked Granny what I should do if Aunt Cora Lee died while I was at her house. She'd just laugh and say that Aunt Cora Lee was going to outlive every one of us.

Aunt Cora Lee was married to Granny's baby brother, Hassell. Uncle Hassell had big ears and thick black glasses. He lost his left leg in a war long before I was born, and he walked with a dark, wooden cane that had notches carved in it. Granny told me not to stare at Uncle Hassell when he walked, but I couldn't help it. The left leg of his trousers was always held up with the biggest safety pin I'd ever seen. I wasn't staring at his missing leg. I just couldn't take my eyes off that shiny pin.

Granny said Uncle Hassell couldn't hear thunder. All day, he and Aunt Cora Lee yelled back and forth to one another from the living room to the kitchen. And all day, I worried that Uncle Hassell was going to fall or Aunt Cora Lee was going to keel over from her coronary.

I once told Granny that I didn't want to stay with Aunt Cora Lee and Uncle Hassell anymore, but she said that was nonsense. She said they loved me, and besides, Aunt Cora Lee may have been a weak old woman, but she made the best zucchini bread in Mississippi. I knew Granny was right about that.

Aunt Cora Lee had dog named Lady Belle. I didn't know what kind of dog it was, but it wasn't the size of a sack of flour. It had short brown hair and its pink tongue was covered in black spots. It didn't much look like a dog, and it sure didn't sound like a dog when it barked. It sounded more like some kind of sick bird squawking, but Aunt Cora Lee assured me that Lady Belle was, indeed, a dog.

Uncle Hassell wasn't too fond of Lady Belle. I once watched the dog pull the safety pin right off Uncle Hassell's trousers. I'd never heard such colorful language come out of an old man's mouth, with the exception of Mr. Wendell Murphy at the general store down the road from my Granny's house. Granny usually left me in the car when she went inside the general store because she said Mr. Wendell "didn't know how to talk around young'uns."

Even though Uncle Hassell hated that dog, Aunt Cora Lee loved Lady Belle. I didn't know why she was so fond of her, either. I'd seen Aunt Cora Lee wiping blood from her hands covered in bumpy blue veins because Lady Belle played a little too rough. I knew that if a coronary didn't kill Aunt Cora Lee, then that Lady Belle sure would.

So Aunt Cora Lee put Lady Belle in the back yard while I was at her house eating zucchini bread and listening to her and Uncle Hassell yell back and forth over the television. She said Lady Belle didn't know me too well, so I might get bit. I knew it didn't matter if she knew me well or not.

Aunt Cora Lee always went back to her bedroom to rest after lunch. I would follow her back to her room because I didn't want to be stuck in the living room with Uncle Hassell. I could never yell loud enough for him to hear me, despite my mama always saying there was a set of lungs on me like no other.

I would watch Aunt Cora Lee slip her white loafers from her curved feet, and she would slide into her bed and cover herself with the bird of paradise quilt. She would place her gold colored glasses on the doily covered nightstand, and she would quickly drift off to sleep.

I would sit in the plush chair beside her bed and read the big stack of children's books that she kept in a wicker basket on the hardwood floor, looking up often to make sure Aunt Cora Lee's chest was moving up and down beneath the colorful quilt.

I often wondered where Aunt Cora Lee had gotten the tattered Little Golden Books. She and Uncle Hassell never had any children, and I was the only kid that ever came around. I noticed little stickers stuck to the back that said "5₵" or sometimes "10₵" for the thicker books. I would pick at the little round stickers, wondering if Aunt Cora Lee had bought the books at a yard sale just for me.

Sometimes Aunt Cora Lee would gasp for breath in her sleep, and my heart would leap from my chest as I prepared to run to Uncle Hassell and loudly scream to him that Aunt Cora Lee was finally dead.

But she never died. Instead, she woke up exactly 57 minutes from the moment that she had gone to sleep. She never winded the Big Ben alarm clock beside the bed, and I never woke her. She always woke up on her own, cleared her throat, sat up in bed and slipped the large round spectacles over her glassy blue eyes.

I could read nearly all of the Little Golden Books in 57 minutes. I was usually left with only one or two pages of "The Pokey Little Puppy" when she woke.

After Aunt Cora Lee's nap, I would follow her back to the kitchen where I helped her dry dishes as she asked me a lot of questions about my mama, my daddy and my granny. Mama always told me to tell Aunt Cora Lee that everything was fine, so I did as I was told.

When I was younger, I gave Aunt Cora Lee information about Mama and Daddy and Granny. I didn't know any better. When she asked if Daddy still drank out of his brown glass bottles after supper, I'd tell her yes. When she asked if Mama had bought a new Sunday dress lately, I'd describe the dress to a t- right down to the pearl buttons. When she asked if Granny had talked about her, I said that Granny thought that all of Aunt Cora Lee's death talk was just for show.

But now that I was ten and Mama had told me that Aunt Cora Lee only asked those questions to be nosey, I didn't give her much information anymore. Daddy did still drink out of his brown glass bottles, Mama was at Lowenstein's getting a new dress every week, and Granny still thought Aunt Cora Lee was a crybaby, but that wasn't any of Aunt Cora Lee's business.

Sometimes Aunt Cora Lee and I would sit on the front porch and watch the few cars that sailed down the sleepy street. We could hear Uncle Hassell's television through the living room walls right out onto the porch, so we'd move to the side porch where it wasn't as loud. I don't know why we didn't just go to the side porch from the get go.

We would sit in old metal chairs, painted mint green, and we'd rock and admire Mrs. Mary Warren's hydrangea bushes. Aunt Cora Lee told me that if Mrs. Mary put acid on the bushes, the petals would turn from blue to pink. That's all we pretty much talked about when we sat on the porch on the side of the house because there wasn't anything else to see. We talked about hydrangeas. And sometimes Lady Belle would start squawking from the back yard, and Aunt Cora Lee would say we needed to go check on her, but we never did. I think we were both too afraid.

Uncle Hassell usually fell asleep over the sound of the booming television while we sat on the porch. We'd come in and Aunt Cora Lee would flip the switch on the set, and the house would fall silent. The only sound you could hear was the breath rustling through Uncle Hassell's nose hairs and the clock ticking on the fireplace mantle.

Aunt Cora Lee liked to knit, but she could only do it from the high back chair in the living room. And she could only knit when the room was nice and quiet. So she would knit while Uncle Hassell sawed logs in his own high back chair, and I grabbed stationery and pencils from the secretary drawer.

I couldn't draw very well. The only thing that I could doodle was a house. I could make a perfect square house with a triangle roof and windows lining the front. I always drew a small window on the front door, just like Aunt Cora Lee's door. There was a storm door on the front of the house, so she kept the heavy wooden door swung open into the living room most of the time. I would look up and admire the stained glass in the small window of the front door, and I would attempt to draw it on Aunt Cora Lee's fancy stationery.

Before long, the storm door would swing open, and my Granny would be standing there, ready to take me back to her farmhouse on the north side of town.

"Well, my word, Lil. You nearly scared me to death," Aunt Cora Lee would say every time.

"Well, Cora Lee, who in the world did you think it was?" Granny would shake her head.

I gathered up the pencils and the stationery and stuffed it all back into the secretary as Granny asked Aunt Cora Lee about our day.

"This pain just won't leave me be, Lil. It's going to be the death of me. I know it is. And this morning I started getting the strangest feeling in my left ear. It's not quite a ringing, but it's a dull kind of sound. I just can't explain it, but it is in my left ear which means it probably has something to do with my heart. You know any kind of pain on the left side can be heart related, Lil. I just don't know if I'll be up for keeping her tomorrow while you go down to the home. I just don't know. I will have to get some good rest tonight or I just don't know."

My Granny had stopped listening to her after the first word or two, and she pulled me to her side and ran her ring-covered fingers through my long, dishwater blonde ponytail.

"Tell Aunt Cora Lee you'll see her tomorrow," Granny said as she pushed the door open and stepped onto the front porch.

"See you tomorrow," I gave Aunt Cora Lee a weak smile, and she returned one of her own, even weaker.

“Bye, Hassell,” Granny loudly called from the front porch as we walked toward the driveway.

Uncle Hassell slept soundly, not even twitching a furry eyebrow, as the storm door slammed behind us.

ELLEN, 1965

You couldn't find a clean storefront window on Main Street in Hatchie County, Tennessee during the cotton picking season. An inch of brown earth rested on the glass windows, concealing the ladies' church dresses and men's fedoras from view.

Most of the fields were on the east side of town, so the cotton pickers came right through the heart of Hatchie County, down Main Street to the Sugar Creek Gin on the west side, leaving a trail of murky dust and white bolls behind. It looked like Christmas with all of the snow on the sidewalks.

I headed out the front door of our old house on Washburn Street with my father's lunch in a paper sack, as my mother called out to me that only a fool would wear a white dress downtown in September. She swore my beautiful A-line dress would be dark as mud by the time I got back home.

The walk to my daddy's jewelry store on Main Street only took a few minutes, and I wanted to look my best for John William Brown should I happen to see him along the way. I loved my white dress. It gleamed against my summer suntanned skin, and it hugged me in all the right places. I would take my chances with the dust.

I shuffled down the alley behind the Shiloh Baptist Church and emerged onto Main Street. I saw a cotton picker coming over the hill by the courthouse, so I jogged across the grimy road littered with cotton and ducked into the jewelry store before the cloud of soil engulfed me.

"Girl, what do you mean wearing that white dress down here in September? It'll be dark as mud by the time you get back home," Mrs. Colby scoffed at me as she dusted the shelves showcasing watches and necklaces in the front window. "Hurry up and shut the door before that picker comes by. It's dustier than my Herbert's plantin' boots in here."

Mrs. Colby had worked for my daddy as long as I could remember. She wasn't the cheeriest lady in town, and she always spoke exactly what was on her mind whether it was polite or not, but she and my grandmother had been the best of friends, and she was like a second mother to my daddy.

"Ellen, is that you?" Daddy stuck his head out from his office at the back of the jewelry store, the loupe still attached to his eye glasses.

"I brought you lunch. A bologna sandwich and some of Mama's pickles," I held up the paper sack and walked toward my handsome daddy as the picker roared by the store and shook the jewelry cases.

"Well, I'll be," Daddy grinned. "You know I usually eat lunch over at Marvin's. Why the special delivery? And in your Sunday best, too."

"I thought I'd be nice, Daddy. What's the crime in that?" I placed the paper sack on Daddy's desk next to his cigars as he sat back down in his leather chair and continued setting a square stone in gold prongs.

"You sure you're not trying to run into some young fellow downtown, are you? Maybe Leon Downey? Have you got your eye on that Downey boy?" Daddy laughed heartily and his belly jiggled as he delicately handled the diamonds.

"There's not a girl in Hatchie County that's got her eye on Leon Downey. He's got a face only a mother could love, and I don't even think his mama is too fond of him," I made a disgusted face as Daddy chuckled.

"Hill, don't you let her talk that way about that Downey boy. Maybe he looks like he's been hit in the kisser with a steam shovel, but he comes from good Christian folks. His mama has a heart of gold. Don't you talk that way about the Downey family, Ellen," Mrs. Colby called from the front of the store as she scattered the dust on the glass shelves with the feathers in her hand.

Daddy laughed and shook his head. "Well, I'm actually glad you stopped by. Seeing as it is Friday, would you run down to the Commerce and Trust and make my deposits? I'd like to get this ring set for Mrs. Hardy as soon as possible. Lord knows she'll pitch a fit if it's not ready to show off at tonight's big D.A.R. meeting."

"Don't you talk about Mrs. Hardy, Hill. She doesn't need her own jeweler talking about her in that way. Maybe she likes to brag now and again, but she doesn't need you talking about her. Lord knows she's got enough people around here flapping their gums about that fancy new Cadillac she's driving, with the dirt barely settled around her husband's grave. Must have been some kind of insurance policy," Mrs. Colby's voice trailed off.

Daddy shook his head. "Will you make my deposits please, Ellen?"

"I guess so," I nodded as Daddy motioned to the stack of deposits on his mahogany desk covered in nicks. I secretly hoped that I would see John William along my route.

"Hurry up now, girl. There's another picker coming. That dress'll be dark as mud by the time you reach the bank," Mrs. Colby shouted as I slammed the door and shuffled to Commerce and Trust on the corner.

I casually looked inside the murky windows of Downey's Hardware Store for a glimpse of John William, but I only saw Leon standing behind the counter with his bulbous nose and cow lick. I made another repulsed face, skipped over a few snowy cotton bolls, and I darted into the air-conditioned bank.

I searched the teller's faces and noticed that John William's mother had the shortest line. I walked toward her, nodding to a few of my mother's friends along the way. I cleared my throat, shifted my weight and stared at the checks in my hand when her strident voice startled me.

"Well, Miss Ellen. Aren't you pretty as a picture in your white dress?" Mrs. Lil smiled at me as I approached her counter and slid the deposits to her.

"Thank you," I spoke softly and looked to the filth on the hem of the dress. My white flats were now beige and soiled.

"How is Mrs. Laney doing with her stomach upset? Is she feeling any better?" Mrs. Lil's ring-covered fingers quickly typed on the adding machine.

"She's much better. Thank you," I said. I always felt so intimidated around Mrs. Lil. She sure was a beautiful woman, with her brown hair in a pretty bun at the nape of her neck. She wore brightly colored lipstick that perfectly matched her fingernail polish. She also wore more jewelry than my mother, the jeweler's own wife.

"We missed her at church Wednesday night. Nobody makes peach cobbler like your mother," Mrs. Lil smiled.

"She just had a little bug. She's fine now. I'll tell her you asked about her, Mrs. Lil," I spoke over the sound of several men standing in the middle of the lobby and laughing heartily with the bank president, Mr. Hunter.

"Have you seen John William today?" Mrs. Lil asked as my heart palpitated at the very sound of his name.

"No mam," I shook my head.

"He didn't help his daddy pick cotton this season. He's been working over at Downey's this summer. Sometimes he stops in here on his lunch break to see me, but I haven't seen a hair on his head this afternoon."

"I didn't see him in Downey's," I cleared my throat while Mrs. Lil wrote out Daddy's deposit slip.

"I certainly hope he's not courting around with that Willard girl. You know the horse man's daughter? Do you know much about her, Ellen?" Mrs. Lil searched my face for answers.

"I don't know her that well, Mrs. Lil. We don't run in the same circle," I felt my stomach turn in knots as I thought about John William and that fast girl holding hands or smoking cigarettes behind Marvin's Diner.

"Well, between us, she seems a little wild to me. I don't like it one bit. I just don't," she spoke quietly and shook her head in disapproval.

"I'm sure she's nice," I lied, wishing that I had the courage to spill to Mrs. Lil the dirty secrets that I'd heard about Caroline Willard and how she'd shown half the boys in the county the birthmark on her inner thigh. She said it looked like West Virginia, but Charlie Mott said it looked like a hopping frog. He even croaked at her when she passed him in the hallway at school.

"Maybe I ought to suggest John William call on you sometime, Ellen? You're such a pretty girl and from such a nice family, too. Your mama is just a peach and your daddy is such a good man. Maybe you're just what John William needs?" she winked at me and handed me the deposit slip.

"Oh, I don't know, Mrs. Lil. I just- I," I became noticeably embarrassed and felt my face turn a warm shade of crimson.

"I didn't mean to make you ill at ease, dear," she reached out and patted my hand resting on the counter as it crumpled the deposit slip.

"Oh, you- you didn't. I-" I pulled my hand away and ran my fingers over the silky ribbon tied around my blonde ponytail.

"Did you hear that we are moving to Mississippi next summer as soon as John William finishes out his senior year?" she changed the subject.

"No mam," I shook my head.

"I've got an older sister down in Itta Bena. She's been sick with the fever for months now, and my brother and his wife just up and left her down there in the middle of that race war. They moved up to Saltillo and left her there, and she's got no one to cook her meals or help her. Even if my brother was still down in Itta Bena with her, he couldn't do much seeing as how he lost his leg in the second war. And my sister-in-law, well she's just useless. She's been sick since the day she was born and God forbid she lifts a weak finger to help Beck.

"I've got to get down there and get her out of that civil rights mess. I've talked John Senior into fixing up my grandparent's old place in Itta Bena, and next summer, hoping Beck makes it that long, we're just going to move her right in there with us and see to her every need. John William is even going to apply to Mississippi College. Won't that be something? John William a college boy?" Mrs. Lil's eyes lit up at the thought of returning to Mississippi.

"That'll be something," I choked on the knot in the back of my throat, wondering what in Heaven I would do without a glimpse of John William at First Methodist on Sunday mornings.

"And maybe I'll get him away from that Willard girl once and for all?" she laughed. "Oh, look at me, boring you to tears. Your daddy is probably waiting on those slips."

"Thank you, Mrs. Lil," I turned from the counter, fighting back the dampness in my eyes and trying to process what I would do without John William sleeping under the same Tennessee stars as me every night.

"If you see John William out there, send him on over, would you, honey?" she called to me as I nodded. "And don't stay on the street too long or that white dress'll turn dark as mud."

I pushed open the glass door and stepped into the dusty humidity, no longer caring if my white dress turned the color of sludge. I was eager to pass by Downey's Hardware again and hopefully catch a glimpse of him this time. I picked up the pace and stepped over some more bolls. As soon as I turned the corner, I saw John William and Caroline Willard stepping out of Downey's and they headed toward the diner.

I clean forgot about Daddy's deposit slips and I raced toward Washburn Street.

MRS. LANEY, 1991

Henry McMillin hadn't been the same since his life-altering loss on *Jeopardy!* in 1974. I watched from my kitchen window as he shuffled around his garden in tube socks and a stained red flannel robe. He haphazardly pruned his roses and mumbled the question that would always haunt him, 'What are the Apennine Mountains?"

I remembered the old man when he was just a boy, calling on my older sister Nance every Sunday after church. He was an awkward young man, so smart that he seemed dumb about the simplest kinds of things. He once explained all of the elements on the Periodic Table to Nance, but he couldn't even properly bait a fishing line.

He never married, staying on with his mother after his daddy died in a car accident on Route 7 back in the fifties. Mr. Patrick McMillin slammed right into a cotton picker one September morning and they found some of his teeth nearly twenty three feet from his Plymouth. At least that's what Sherriff Tucker told all the boys down at the pool hall.

I visited Henry and his mother, Mrs. Rose, quite a bit after Mr. Patrick died. I'd sit at their kitchen table with both of my little girls in tow, and we'd have a cup of coffee or a cinnamon roll. I always wondered how in the world someone as beautiful and debonair as Rose McMillin had such an oddball boy.

Mrs. Rose lived on nearly twenty years after Mr. Patrick passed, listening to Henry McMillin talk intelligently about amphibians and planets and whatnot, all the while he could barely sweep the front stoop correctly. When Nance and her husband came down from Nashville for a visit, I'd catch Henry peering at her from his bedroom window while she sipped sweet tea on the back porch. She'd notice him staring once in a while, too, and in typical Nance fashion, she'd give him a teasing little wave and Henry would disappear behind his curtains.

I was all alone now that Nance was out of her mind and wasting away in a Veteran's Home up in Nashville and my own husband was six feet in the ground, his lungs riddled with emphysema, his bones turning to dust. My oldest daughter, Ellen, had married a gambler and moved to New Orleans when she was only 18. My youngest left home when she was 21, and no one heard a word from her since. I was all alone to watch crazy Henry McMillin butcher his roses and mumble answers in the form of questions.

I still went to First Methodist every Sunday and baked peach cobblers for the Ladies Auxiliary Club on Tuesdays. I watered the impatiens and the azalea bushes every morning and mopped the kitchen floor after dinner. Sometimes Ellen would call, her voice slurred from the alcohol and her womb empty as the day she was born, and I'd act like a visitor had come knocking on the door just so I could hang up the phone.

When Dorothy Turner called my line one Sunday afternoon asking if I had any ironing that needed to be done, I watched Henry from my kitchen window as he shuffled around his backyard and I told her no. That didn't stop her from showing up on my stoop on Washburn Street just before I headed to the evening services down at First Methodist.

Dorothy was a young black girl in her late twenties. Her eyes were the darkest hazel I'd ever seen and her hair was in the tightest bun. I just knew that it must hurt to wear hair pulled back so tightly. Even her eyebrows were raised from the pull.

I knew Dorothy's grandmother, Della, from years before. She lived in an unpainted house by the railroad tracks with her husband and a house full of young'uns. When my husband, Hill, and I went down to the fish market on Thursday nights, I would see little Dorothy playing alone on the tracks in her tattered dresses and holey shoes and I prayed for her safety. Seems her hair was pulled tight even all those years ago.

Della helped a friend of mine, Mrs. Lil Brown, when her family packed and moved down to Mississippi in 1966. Mrs. Lil said Della had carefully wrapped all of her breakables in newspaper. She said she'd wrapped all those breakables it in an intricate manner, with corners tucked in tightly so that the glass was safe. I wondered why she was so careful with the white lady's china but she didn't seem to mind her little grandbaby playing on railroad tracks.

So I asked Della Turner to pack up and clean out my youngest daughter's room when she left with no sign of ever returning because I just couldn't bear to do it. Dorothy's grandmother did an excellent job, as she chewed on tobacco and even wiped tears from her dark eyes once or twice as she folded my girl's dresses and carefully placed them in a cardboard box.

Della came back in 1975 when Hill died. I let her take some of his Sunday suits and shirts to her husband. She told me I didn't owe her any money for the rest of her work. She helped me off and on throughout the years until she passed away, too.

When Dorothy showed up on my stoop that muggy Sunday afternoon in the late eighties, begging me to let her iron my laundry, she said her grandmama had always spoken kindly of me. She said her grandmama had always felt a sadness for me since my youngest daughter disappeared.

I didn't want to let Dorothy do my ironing. If I gave her my ironing then that would leave me nothing to do on Monday morning. I looked forward to the small pile of wrinkled clothes that waited for me on Monday morning. When you're 65 with no one to talk to and your only entertainment is watching a crazy man murder bushes and mumble to himself, then ironing seems like an escape. Ironing, mending, cleaning, polishing my old jewels- it all kept me busy. It all kept my mind occupied.

I continued to tell her I didn't need her services, but Dorothy said she'd taken on her sister's baby to raise. She told me that her fiancé was too sick to work, her sister too lazy and she needed whatever change I could spare. That new baby needed diapers, and I guess I needed some ironing done. I told her to come back on Monday. And she came back every Monday for years.

"That old Henry is out there killing them bushes again today, Mrs. Laney. Got 'em all pruned down to sticks. They ain't nothing but sticks," Dorothy said as she walked through my back door one muggy August morning.

She hung her purse on the hook by the refrigerator, and she walked back to the laundry room to get the iron and the board.

"He's a fool, Dorothy. He's just a damned old fool," I sat at the kitchen table and concentrated on the crossword puzzle.

She returned to the kitchen and set up the board in front of the pantry door. She plugged in the iron and got straight to work, humming her familiar old gospel songs and occasionally glancing at Henry out the kitchen window.

In only ten minutes, she'd finished ironing my laundry- three dresses, a white button down and gray slacks that I wore to the Auxiliary Club on Tuesdays. I told her she could pull a couple of Hill's old shirts out of his drawer and iron them for the heck of it.

"What ever happened to your youngest, Mrs. Laney?" she asked as she sprayed starch on one of the dress shirts that hadn't been worn in nearly 15 years.

"I don't quite know, Dorothy," I squinted through my glasses at the crossword puzzle. "She left home one afternoon and never came back."

"I remember hearing about that when I was a young one. Grandmama kept me in the house for nearly a week because the whole town thought a kidnapper done got on the loose," Dorothy remembered aloud as she soaked the shirt in starch.

"But she let you play on the tracks, Dorothy. I remember you playing on those tracks. Your feet could have gotten caught in the rails, Dorothy. They sure could've," I scribbled a three letter word in the small boxes.

"What you think happened to her, Mrs. Laney? Mother's tuition, they call it?" she placed Hill's crisp shirt on the wire hanger and hung it from the doorframe in the kitchen.

"Intuition, Dorothy, and I don't know. She went by her daddy's jewelry store. She helped Mrs. Colby dust a few shelves and figure the books. She told her daddy she was walking back home and we never saw her again," I erased the wrong three letter word and tried to think of another one.

"My Lord, Mrs. Laney. That's some kind of hurt, ain't it? Not knowing what happened to your baby like that?" Dorothy shook her head and took another wrinkled shirt from the pile on the kitchen counter.

"Well, I've grown used to it, I suppose," I tapped the pencil to my temple.

"You thinking she's still alive, Mrs. Laney? How old would she be now? I remember my grandmama all worried and crying because that poor girl went missing. You think she's still alive?"

"She'd be 40 now, Dorothy. I'm pretty sure she's alive somewhere. She just didn't want to be here anymore I guess," I gave up on the three letter word and moved to another clue on the puzzle.

"You ever try to find her, Mrs. Laney? You get one of them secret service men or something to go looking for her? You should have done that," she said as steam rose from the iron.

"I called in a private investigator from Memphis a couple of times. Hill insisted I keep on paying that fat man to look for her, but she was long gone by then. I suspect she went out west somewhere. She had asthma. We always said she'd breathe better out west. I suspect that's where she went," I studied the clue as the iron hissed and the stout smell of starch filled my nostrils.

"And Miss Ellen? Where'd she go? Why she didn't come home after her sister done left you, Mrs. Laney?"

"I'll say, Dorothy, dear. Are you trying to get me upset? Is that what you're trying to do?" I peered at Dorothy from under my bifocals, her dark skin sweating from the iron's steam. An ashamed look came across her face.

"Well, no, mam. I'm sorry, Mrs. Laney. I've just always been curious about your situation is all. I didn't mean no harm in it," she shook her head and lifted the iron from the stiff shirt.

"I know you didn't. I know you're curious. I suppose all of Hatchie County has been curious about my family for the last twenty years. I've had plenty of pitiable looks thrown my way, my share of pats on the back," I sat the pencil on the wooden table and fiddled with the diamond on my finger. "If Hill hadn't smoked those damned cigars one after the other, he'd probably still be setting stones on Main Street. If Ellen hadn't lost all her self-esteem during her teenage years, she wouldn't have run off with that no- good gambler that never gave her any children. I'm sure if Hill and I hadn't been so strict on my youngest after Ellen left, well, she'd probably be right here, and there'd be no need for you to be asking all these questions."

"I'll be, Mrs. Laney. I didn't mean to-" Dorothy stuttered.

"I know you didn't. I'm sure she'd be right here if," I removed my glasses and wiped my eyes before the first tear could fall, "if we hadn't been so hard on her. If my oldest girl hadn't gotten caught up with that Cajun riff raff, we wouldn't have been so tough on my baby girl. We just wanted to protect her. If Ellen hadn't- we wouldn't. She had asthma. I bet she can breathe better out west. It's dry out west."

"Oh, Mrs. Laney, you've gone and got upset, ain't you? I didn't mean for it. I sure didn't," Dorothy watched me from the other side of the ironing board, wondering whether or not to come to my side and console me.

"Nonsense," I cleared my throat, composed myself and placed my glasses back on my face. "Let's talk about something else now, okay? Put that iron away, fix us both a cup of coffee, and tell me about your nephew's first day of school."

CAROLINE, 1966

My daddy was known for many things. He liked being known as "the horse man out on Route 8" the best. If a foal couldn't get born, my daddy could get it born. If a mare had a hoof abscess, my daddy could drain it, blindfolded, with the cigarette still hanging from his lips. He knew all there was to know about horses, all right. We were too poor to keep any horses of our own, but Daddy grew up with horses. He could patch them up real good and quite a few times, men would load their sick horses onto a trailer and bring them out to our shack on Route 8 so my daddy could take a look at them.

There was a time when my daddy was wealthy, a time when he wasn't ashamed to walk down the street. Those were the days before he was also known as a bum, a cheater and a drunk. Yep, Daddy liked being known as "the horse man out on Route 8" the best.

My daddy's pa knew all there was to know about horses, too. He bought them and sold them and bred them on his 1200 acre farm in north Hatchie County. Grandpa came from good people. His daddy had killed 23 Yankees in the Civil War and they owned half the soil in the county, and no one was more respected around here than war heroes and cotton farmers.

My daddy was raised up on that horse farm. He was raised up to be a good man, too, but he couldn't withstand the temptation of whiskey and women. He spent so much time and money on both that he didn't have any left over for his wife and daughter, and years before my grandpa had died and left his fortune to my daddy's two brothers, he said my daddy didn't belong to him no more.

No one remembers my bloodline when they see me. No one remembers the dead Yankees or the cotton empire or the pure bred horses or the wealth. When they see me, they see my daddy stepping out of the pool hall with his glassy eyes and his dirty clothes. They see him stumbling about town, asking for odd jobs, begging for rides to Crawley County to get some cheap liquor and even cheaper women. They see my mama's tattered dresses and bruised cheeks because my daddy got drunk and she said something stupid. Townspeople look at me and see my pitiful parents. My parents are what make people's opinions of me.

But all that didn't stop John William Brown from calling on me one June day. My daddy's reputation didn't stop John William from taking me to the picture show or fishing down at Howard's Pond. It didn't stop him from holding my hand and telling me that my brown eyes were the most beautiful he'd ever seen. Nope, it didn't stop him one bit.

I could see the way people looked at me on John William's arm. They grimaced, they scowled; they appeared to have seen something blasphemous. I knew we didn't make sense to them, but we made perfect sense to us.

I didn't have a need for whiskey like my daddy. I didn't want to wear old rags like my mama. I wanted to get back to my old bloodline of Yankee killers and cotton farmers and the only way I could get there was with John William. That don't mean I didn't love John William. That don't mean that I was only with him so I can be somebody. No, I loved John William just fine. I loved the way he made me laugh and the way he kissed the nape of my neck. I loved John William Brown just fine.

John William's mama wouldn't ever admit it, but she had her eye on my uncle in their younger days. When she and John William's daddy were first married, they moved from Itta Bena, Mississippi to Hatchie County to tend to John William's grandmama. My daddy said there she was, the newlywed Lillian Odie Brown, nearly every afternoon in the winter months, walking by the Willard Farm while John Senior was feeding his mama medicine and praying she'd live another day. Mrs. Lil said she walked by to admire the gold and white horses, but they all knew she admired Uncle Albie. But, no, she'd never admit that now days. Even though Uncle Albie is still a well- respected man in this county, and they nod to one another in passing at the country club, she'd never admit Uncle Albie was a fine gentleman to John William, just because Uncle Albie's some kin to me.

"You know I'm going to be moving in two days, Caroline," John William spoke over the croaking of bullfrogs as we sat on his winding front porch one July night.

"I can't bear it, John William. I can't bear not being with you," I wiped my watering eyes, not wanting to hear this conversation, not wanting to hear him talk about being dead-set on leaving.

"My Aunt Beck is awful sick. If Mama doesn't get down to Itta Bena and tend to her, she's going to be awful sick, too. Mama can't stay up here in Tennessee with her sister in so much need, with heated marches right outside her door, and I can't talk her out of it. That's just what we are going to do. Dad has been going back and forth to Itta Bena to fix up her grandparent's old farmhouse. He's damn near remodeled the whole thing. It's really beautiful down there, Caroline. There are acres upon acres of rolling land, and the biggest whitetail I've ever seen walks right up to the back porch. Mama is set on going," he held my hand as we sat on the painted steps.

"We're both done with school now. Why can't we just make a life for ourselves somewhere? Why do *you* have to go?" I begged him and rested my head on the shoulder of his white t-shirt.

"Mama and Dad both have their hearts set on me going to Mississippi College, Caroline. I've got my heart set on it, too. I can do big things if I get that kind of education. I could practice law. I've got to go with them, too. There's no way around it. That's what I need to do," he nodded his head. "It's a wonderful opportunity."

"I wish Mrs. Lil cared for me a little bit. If she cared for me, she wouldn't mind me coming along, but she looks at me the way the rest of this town looks at me. All they see is Stanley Willard's daughter. I'm the horse man's daughter. I'm the drunks' girl. That's all anyone around here will ever see," I sighed and lifted my head from his shoulder.

"My mama is set in her thinking and I can't help that, but you've got to quit worrying about what these other Hatchie hypocrites think of you. You're good as gold in my eyes. That's what matters," John William lifted my hand to his face and softly kissed my knuckles.

"I won't ever amount to nothing around here. You've got to take me with you. Can't you take me with you?" I pleaded with him, nervous that his mama and daddy would pull up any moment in their big red Deville and catch me, white trash, on the front porch steps of their beautiful country home.

"I can't take you, Caroline," he shook his head and squeezed my hand. "But I'll be back for you. I can promise you that."

"When will you be back? Am I supposed to wait on you for five years, maybe ten? You think I can make it here that long? I'll be an old woman by then," I became angry with him and dropped his hand.

"Hell, Caroline, I don't mean ten years. I'll be done with school before then. I will come for you as soon as I'm done. We'll pack you up and move to Biloxi. You like Biloxi? You like the Gulf?" he smiled warmly at me.

"You know I ain't ever seen the Gulf. How'd I know if I like it or not?" I whined.

"You'd like it just fine," he pulled me close to him, my yellow dress, damp from the humidity, clinging to my legs.

"I'd better go before your parents get back. I'm sure bingo is over by now," I stood to my feet, my dress full of wrinkles.

John William grasped me in his arms one last time and his warm mouth covered mine. I pulled away and buried my face into his sweaty neck. I closed my eyes and tried to memorize the feeling of his arms around me.

I finally pushed him away and avoided his green eyes. I didn't want him to see my eyes, either, wet with salty tears. I didn't want him to see how much of a hold he had on me. He stood beneath the porch light, moths swarming his dark hair, as I stepped down and walked toward the back of his house.

"I'll meet you at the diner for lunch tomorrow?" he called to me as I stopped and turned to look at him.

"I'm helping Mama mend some dresses tomorrow. I don't know if I'll have time to get away," I shrugged as the warm wind blew through the mossy trees above my head.

"When then, Caroline? I leave day after tomorrow," he stuffed his hands in the pockets of his blue jeans and stared at me from the porch.

"I guess never," I inhaled sharply and hoped it would hold the tears from streaming down my tan cheeks.

"Caroline," he looked to his feet, "I don't know what to- I don't know."

"Write me your new phone number if you get some time. I'll give you a call once in a while when I'm downtown by the payphone," I replied in a sharp way.

"Caroline," he sighed.

"Bye, John William," I snapped.

I walked quickly toward the field behind his house, hoping my angry tone would send him running for me, send him after me, to grab me and kiss me and tell me I could come with him. He'd demand to his parents that I stay in the guest room in the Odie farmhouse in Itta Bena, Mississippi, and that I would help Mrs. Lil care for his Aunt Beck, and that one day, we'd be married, and that's just the way it was going to be. I turned around to look for him, to see him running for me with his arms outstretched and his eyes damp, but all I saw was the shadow of his house in the moonlight.

The full moon lit my way as I paced along the side of the cotton field. I kicked at the dirt clods beneath my dingy, worn-out flats and wiped the stray damp hairs that had fallen from my ponytail and stuck to my sweaty forehead.

Every time I snuck away from John William's house and walked this path to my place on Route 8, I had wondered if it would be my last time to tread this trail. I always knew that Mrs. Lil was liable to forbid John William from ever seeing me again. I always knew John William was bound to fall in love with another girl. He could have his pick in the entire county- the doctor's girl, the banker's girl, the jeweler's girl. He could have any one of them, with their expensive polished cotton dresses and their shiny blonde hair tied up in ribbons and their sweet smiles and rich daddies. I knew it was just a matter of time before he threw me over for one of those beauties. Mrs. Lil would certainly approve of that decision.

But he never did. He never heeded Mrs. Lil's advice to drop me for one of those socially acceptable girls. For a year, I continued to walk this field road from Route 8 to the Brown house. Now John William was leaving for Mississippi, and this walk from his property would be my last one. He'd be leaving the land where his father was born, where he was raised, where we'd held one another close while his parents were off playing bingo under the big red tent by the Presbyterian Church. He'd be a college boy, like my daddy's brother's boys- just like my rich king cotton thoroughbred cousins, with their Chevrolet convertibles and college education. John William was destined to be just like them, and just like my cousins, he'd have no use for me.

I knew that he'd never come back for me. I'd never see Biloxi or the ocean. I'd never take John William's last name or eat at Mrs. Lil's Thanksgiving table. I'd never be good enough for his family. He'd fall in love with some rich college girl, with her fat politician daddy and her bloodline of Yankee killers, and I'd be forgotten.

But maybe one day, when John William Brown was an old man living in his mansion by the Gulf of Mexico, he'd drink too much gin and he'd have a distant memory of some poor Tennessee girl with a wild reputation, with dark hair that tangled in the humidity, with dark eyes that reminded him of cocoa, with hand-me-down dresses that Coppedge Creek Baptist Church had left on her un-swept front porch in a weathered cardboard box. He'd struggle to remember her name, but it'd never come to him.

He'd just remember that she was some drunken horse man's daughter.

STANLEY WILLARD

I've spent most of my life knowing God was mad at me. I ain't a man of no convictions. I know right from wrong and good from bad. I know I ain't been making God happy with my ways.

I wasn't called to be much. He hadn't called me to be a preacher or a healer. I wasn't meant to walk all His valleys and preach the Gospel. I wasn't meant to baptize the cripples in the river. God hadn't expected that much of me when He drew me up out of dust. All He expected me to do was the right thing, the good thing, but I couldn't hardly ever do it.

When I was a boy, I thought God had some kind of favor on me. I came from good folks, and my mama said this was God's doing. She'd said He put me in a big house with rich land and good people. My grandpa had killed 23 Yankees. We owned half the damn county. Our cotton crop was one of the largest this side of the Mississippi River. Our horses were the purest bred in the state. God put me in a good place, and He expected me to do what I was supposed to do to stay in that good place, but I sure messed that up.

I had my first drink when I was twelve. My daddy gave it to me on our front porch as we sat in matching white rocking chairs and looked across our emerald rolling hills. Daddy said it was aged whiskey, and it cost nearly as much as the beautiful, bulky dining table that Mama set each night for supper.

I was a handsome twelve-year-old boy, wearing fine looking clothes, and I knew a lot of things that most twelve-year-old boys didn't know. I had a pretty good education, I had neat penmanship, and I had a colored woman draw my bath each night. I thought this is what I was supposed to do. I was supposed to drink rich whiskey like gentlemen do.

My pa was a gentleman, and he liked a nice glass of bourbon and a cigar after a long day counting his money and tending to the horses. Drinking was a reward for him. That's all. And he thought it would be a reward for me, too. He didn't know his mistake in giving me that costly poison when I was twelve. It wasn't going to be a reward for me. It was going to be a requirement.

By the time I reached eighteen, I was so far gone with my requirements that my pa threw me out of the old plantation home on the cool green hill. He said I could live out in the barn with the Palominos. I spent a week sleeping in that barn, drinking water from the horse trough, drinking whiskey from my flask and eating horse grain from the muddy ground. I was so engulfed in the smell of mare manure that I was sure I'd never get the stench from my nose. When I couldn't take it anymore, I went back up to the house and begged my mama and daddy to let me in. They both stood on the porch, a shotgun under my daddy's arm, and they banished me from the family. I told them that I'd stay off the bottle, but they returned inside, shutting the door, and I knew I's dead to them. I started off walking only to turn back once to see my brothers, Albie and Jerold, watching me from the dining room window, a blank look on both their faces. I couldn't tell whether they was happy or sad to see me go.

I walked for hours, and then I hitched a ride with a poor farm boy that'd had his arm blown off in the second war. He dropped me off at a tavern on a dirt road in Boll Creek, right across from the state penitentiary. I had fourteen dollars to my name, and I stayed drunk for a few days, watching busloads of new inmates filing into the pen. I washed dishes for pennies and beer at the tavern for the owner, an old half-blind guy named Erskine.

On the third or fourth day of my binge, my head throbbing and my ribs poking through my tattered shirt, Patsy Eldad walked into the tavern. I was drunker than a coon hound and I saw a woman with somewhat delicate features and wide hips that I knew would bear good young'uns. She put her arms around my waist and steadied me enough to walk down to her dirt-floored shack that sat on the east side of the pen. Her mama fixed me up a cot by the stove and she fed me hominy and hog jowl.

When I finally sobered up, I couldn't bear to look at her. If I hadn't been so damn drunk, I wouldn't have given Patsy a second glance. She had a bump on the bridge of her nose, and her child bearing hips were awful manly, but that didn't stop me from sleeping on that cot and drinking enough to make her look pretty again. Before I knew it, I was married to that ugly girl with square hips. When we spoke our vows to some sweaty preacher on a patch of worn down grass in Patsy's yard, I knew that Willard boys ain't supposed to marry dirt poor girls from Boll Creek. I ain't a man of no convictions, but convictions ain't stopped me from doing much.

I couldn't find work in Boll Creek. I held onto the hope that my pa would let me back in my rightful fortune one day, even though I'd married so poorly, so Patsy and I hitched a ride back to Hatchie County and set up in a rundown place on Route 8. I got money here and there doing odd jobs around town, and everyone I came across wanted to know why I, Stanley

Willard, had settled out in a dump on Route 8 with a dirty old girl. They all wanted to know why I wasn't up on the north side of the county, tending to horses and having colored women draw my baths. They all knew the answer, but that didn't stop them from asking.

One time I saw my brother, Jerold, downtown while I's painting the red door on the First Methodist Church. He had one of those pretty Whitman girls on his arm, and when he saw me, he rushed her into the jewelry store just so he wouldn't have to introduce us. He probably had to shell out a small fortune on diamonds for the Whitman girl just so he could avoid me. I knew right then that the blank look on his face a year or so before as he peered out the dining room window was a look of relief that I's finally gone. There's no room for black sheep on a million dollar horse farm in king cotton country.

I'd lost all hope in most things. I knew I's destined to be a drunk and married to an ugly broad and that God had given up on me ever doing right, but when Patsy gave birth to my girl some time later, I looked in that baby's brown eyes and knew that God had given me another chance. I knew He mustn't have been too mad at me because He gave me something so special as a little baby girl, so I told Him, right there in the bedroom while Doctor Parker stitched up Patsy, that I wouldn't let liquor pass through my lips again.

I rushed straight away to the horse farm in an old truck that I'd fixed up. I nearly skipped onto the white porch and I proudly leaned against one of the columns as I told Daddy and my older brother, Albie, that they needn't worry about me drinking no more. I told them that the baby had changed my life. I told Daddy he could let me back on at the farm, that he could put me back in the will, but he said he didn't want no part of that. He said Rome wasn't built in a day and he said that God ain't changed nothing in me.

I left my daddy's house and drove straight on into town, with the intent to find some steady work. I asked Mr. Downey if I could help at the hardware store. I asked Marvin if I could clean tables or cook burgers at the diner. Marvin told me I couldn't cook burgers with shaking hands.

Nobody around here gives you any kind of second chance. I meant what I said when I told the Lord that I didn't intend to drink no more once Caroline was born. I'd stay faithful to Patsy and not bother with those whores and their cheap moonshine over in Crawley County. I'd walk the line and stay on the straight and narrow. All I needed was my daddy to believe in me, or hell, even Mr. Downey or Marvin. When I didn't get encouragement from anyone, I figured God must not have any part in anything with me no more.

I thought that surely He'd put something good in my path once I tried to do right by Him. I thought He'd soften my pa's heart a little or let those men downtown do the right Christian thing and give me some labor, but He didn't. I was determined to do right and I still got shot down, as if I had walked in there stone drunk.

Patsy told me I ought to give it some time. She said that God takes His time sometimes. She said she'd need some time to trust me again, too, after all the wrong things I'd done to her. I knew God wasn't going to change her mind either. God wasn't going to change anyone's mind about me, so why should I change anything I's doing anyway?

I didn't drink on that Saturday or Sunday after Caroline was born, but my hands were shaking so bad that I couldn't even hold my new baby girl. My old truck was out of gas so I walked over to Mr. Starr's on Route 5. I mowed his lawn for a few bucks and then I hitched a ride to Crawley County to reward myself for being on the straight and narrow all weekend.

BECK ODIE, 1945

As I leaned against the side of my father's old Ford truck and crunched the auburn and burgundy leaves beneath my shoes, I glanced over at Mama. I could see the joy on her face that autumn had finally come.

Mama was a large woman and sweat poured down her brow at every opportunity. From April until October, she'd sit on the back porch with a glass of iced tea and a homemade cardboard fan, and she'd fuss about the heat.

"Heat comes straight from the devil, it does. The South gets a glimpse of hell in the summer months, it does," she'd mumble as she wiped her forehead with her apron. Then she'd ask one of us kids to count down the days until relief would come.

The short, hard curls that framed her round face weren't damp with sweat anymore. She could bear to wear her favorite small bell hat when her hair wasn't soaked. Her brow was dry. Her son was returning. Her smile was returning. Mama looked and felt happier than I'd seen her in a long time.

My gaze shifted from my jolly mother sitting on the bed of the truck to my tall, thin father talking with a group of men on the stoop of the drug store. He wore his finest, yet oldest, black suit, with the padded shoulders and wide lapels. He laughed heartily and slapped Sammy Wilkins on the back and then he pulled the pouch of tobacco from his coat pocket.

I always thought Mama and Daddy made an odd looking couple, with Mama being wider than she was tall and Daddy being a mere beanpole. But they were a passionate couple, always showing their affection in front of us, in front of all of Itta Bena. I wanted what they had. I may have been skinny like my daddy, but I'd settle down with a wide man if I could just have a love that mirrored my parent's love.

My younger sister, Lillian, had just married in August. Mama sweat like a field hand during the ceremony as she fanned herself and told Mrs. Emma Lou Barger that fate had played a hand in Lil's marriage. Fate had sent a man all the way from Tennessee to our small Mississippi town to not only work on the railroad, but to fall in love with my sister.

Lil and John were moving back to Tennessee in just a few days. My baby sister was hitched before me. I knew she'd probably be with child in no time at all. I was destined to be an old maid, to be my mama's helper when the scorching summer months were upon us and she was too hot to make my daddy's favorite cornbread. I'd probably stay on with them for the rest of my days. I hung my head and twisted my brown wedge into the crisp leaves.

"What you thinking on, Beck?" Lil's strident voice interrupted my thoughts as she walked toward us. She kissed Mama on her cool cheek and then stood next to me and Daddy's truck.

"I wonder how Hassell is going to be. You know, in his mind? You think his mind is all right?" I pulled an Old Gold from the front pocket on my sage dress.

"I'm not too sure, Beck," Lillian sighed. "There's no telling what he's seen over there in that God-forsaken place."

"He's going to be just fine, girls. My baby boy is going to be all right, he is. He's a strong boy. No war and no loss of limbs is going to put him down. He's going to be just fine, he is," Mama interrupted our conversation in a sure tone, as she swayed her thick legs over the back of the truck and gripped her small clutch purse to her bosom.

"Of course he is, Mama. Don't you worry a bit," Lil reassured her, and then she passed me a doubtful look.

I lit the cigarette and caught a glimpse of Cora Lee Hepler as she held a small American flag in her weak hands and rested against the "Welcome Home" banner that she had draped along the back of her daddy's Buick.

"Look at that ole sad sack, Cora Lee Helpless. She looks like she might faint any minute now. She's only 20-years-old and she is strictly for the birds," Lillian took the cigarette from my hand and put it to her lips.

"Why is she so sickly all of the time?" I wondered aloud.

"She ain't no sicker than you or me. She just wants attention is all. When Hassell first went over to that God-forsaken place, she loved all the pity that came her way. I heard her just a few weeks ago over at Mr. Dooley's store. She was in there all teary-eyed, telling Mr. Dooley's youngest girl, Vivian, that she couldn't sleep nights for worrying if Hassell was dead in some ditch in the jungle. Then she said all that lack of sleep ain't helping her pleurisy none. That child doesn't have pleurisy and I bet she's sleeping just fine, too. I think she-"

Mama interrupted. "Lillian Odie Brown, you hush your mouth. That Cora Lee loves your brother, and she's a mighty fine girl. She lost her own mother when she was just a baby. Why do you talk about her in that way? She will do your brother right, she will. She'll marry him and do him right, she will," Mama said in her sharpest tone as the cool wind swept over her and the floral collar around her neck flapped in the breeze.

“I’m sorry, Mama,” Lillian apologized and handed the cigarette back to me.

“She’s all right, Lillian,” I agreed with Mama.

“Look at this crowd that showed up to see our baby brother home. Our brother, the war hero,” Lillian spoke softer so Mama couldn’t eavesdrop anymore. “It’s half of Itta Bena, Mississippi-all twenty of us.”

“Itty Bitty, Mississippi,” I sighed as I surveyed the small crowd of people lining Main Street. Even the Winchester brothers had shined up their bugles, and they stood in front of Mr. Bennett’s fruit stand, which was now boarded up tighter than a tick. They held the polished instruments in their young hands, waiting on the truck that would bring Hassell over the Roebuck Lake Bridge and straight into town, waiting to strike up some patriotic tune.

In June we received the letter from Okinawa that Hassell had lost his leg. He’d been in the infirmary for nearly a month before he even wrote to us. He didn’t want to discuss the specifics. He just said, “They got my leg, Ma. It was blown clean off, left to rot in the mud.”

Hassell had always been an athletic boy, playing nearly every sport he could in school and his spare time. His legs were strong, they were fast, and his speed is what prompted him to join the forces in the first place. He said if he couldn’t shoot the enemy dead, he could sure outrun them. We all knew it was true.

Daddy took the letter out to the Hepler house on Highway 7, and I sat in the truck watching Cora Lee gasp and nearly faint as she read Hassell’s words.

“They got his leg, Mr. Claiborne. My God in Heaven, they got his leg,” she reached for my father and left his worn shirt damp with tears.

Daddy awkwardly patted her bony shoulder and glanced over at me sitting wide-eyed in his truck. He gave me a shrug, and I shrugged right back to him and then we chuckled at Cora Lee’s dramatics on the ride home.

The whole town knew that Hassell would return without his leg. When he left a few years before, 17-years-old, only Mama, Daddy, Lillian, Cora Lee and I stood at the train station to see him off. Now that he was coming home, half the town was standing there, anticipating his arrival. Mama and Daddy both said it was because he was a war hero - because the people wanted to show him the respect that he deserved, but I knew most of them were there just to see how he would hobble out of the truck that brought him home.

I watched my brother-in-law, John Brown, walk across the bridge in his gray Sunday suit as the north wind blew his jet black hair into his green eyes. He smoothed it down with his palm as he approached Daddy and shook his hand. They exchanged a laugh and then he walked over to Mama and wrapped his arms around her neck.

"Mrs. Texana," he pressed his clean shaven face into her cheek. "You look as beautiful as always and smell fresher than a daisy to boot."

Mama laughed enthusiastically and her round cheeks turned a shade of pink.

"A handsome devil is what you are, John Brown, and sweet as sugar, too. Lillian, how'd you get such a handsome, sweet boy?" Mama smiled at Lillian.

"Fate, Mama. That's what you say, ain't it?" Lillian grinned at her attractive husband as he let go of mother and made his way to me.

"And sweet Beck, are you just as excited as these two ladies to see your baby brother?" he softly grazed my arm with his strong hand.

"I am," I said quietly.

"How do I look? Do I look suitable enough to meet my love's little brother for the first time?" he took a step back and dusted the sleeves of his jacket.

"You look fine, John," I cleared my throat as he took his place beside Lillian and wrapped his fingers around hers freshly painted in peach nail polish.

He began to speak again when the bugles interrupted him and sounded loudly to the tune of "Reveille". Mama jumped from the flat bed, and the truck bounced and the tires rolled slightly. Daddy rushed to her side as she pulled the handkerchief from her purse and leaned into the street to see the green Chevrolet roll over the bridge.

"I see him, Claiborne! I see him!" she began waving her handkerchief in the air.

Lillian and John both hurried to her side, nearly spilling into the street, and I eased up slowly and caught a glimpse of my baby brother's face in the passenger side of the truck, his smile wide, his hand waving quickly out the window to us.

I thought of Cora Lee in that moment and I turned my head toward her. She gripped her daddy's arm as tears streamed down her cheeks and the small flag slowly waved in her frail hands.

"She might just faint, might'n she? I bet she will, Beck. Let's make a bet. Cora Lee Helpless is going to faint right here on Main Street in Itty Bitty, Mississippi," Lillian nudged my arm and nodded at Cora Lee.

The truck stopped right in front of the Hepler Buick with the "Welcome Home" banner proudly draped across the trunk and the door opened.

"You'd think he'd have the driver stop the truck down here with us, wouldn't you? We're his family. That Cora Lee can't take this kind of excitement. I bet she'll just faint. She's just eating this up, half the town watching him greet her before his own mama," Lillian spoke loudly over the noisy bugles.

"Leave them be, Lil. She's waited on him for three years. You'd be in the same state of mind if you hadn't seen John in three years now wouldn't you?" I asked her.

Lillian shrugged as the truck door opened and Hassell's right leg swung onto the street. He turned his torso, held onto the frame of the truck, and he placed a set of wooden crutches on the cracked asphalt. He lifted his body onto the crutches, and for the first time, I saw my brother without both of his legs. The left leg of his green trousers was folded up and secured with a shiny safety pin.

"Mama, are you all right?" Lillian asked when we all looked upon him there, crippled and hobbling towards Cora Lee.

"I'm just fine," Mama wiped her wet eyes as the sound of the bugles suddenly ceased but the silence was met with the clapping and cheers of the townspeople. "I'm fine, all right."

Cora Lee fell limp into Hassell's arms, her own tears washing the rouge from her cheeks, as he dropped the crutches to his side and stood there, holding her, on one leg.

"He should've hugged you first, Mama," Lillian grunted.

"Shut your mouth, Lillian Odie Brown. That's his love. Just like John is your love. Just like your daddy is mine. That's fate," Mama leaned her large frame against Daddy's thin silhouette.

I pulled my warm coat close to my body and let the tears fall.

DELLA, 1972

I ain't seen as much rain in Hatchie County, Tennessee as I did in April of 1972. I'd lived my whole life right here, all 62 years of it, and I'd seen a whole lot of rain. When I's just a girl, I'd watched the low-layin' cotton field behind our house on Route 8 fill up like a dang lake. When I's older, I'd run out front of the house where I lived now to scoop up babies- either my babies or my baby's babies- and save them from the water that suddenly poured out of the sky, poured right out of nowhere while the sun was still a-shinin'. I'd rushed out back to get the clothes off the line when it came down in sheets in all the springtime months, but I ain't never seen as much rain in Hatchie County, Tennessee as I did in April 1972.

I ain't been sittin' on the front porch for more than a few minutes when thunder bellowed and the sky began to pour water. I saw Lula Perkins running across the road from the fish market. She ran straight for my house with a newspaper over her dark head and a sack of catfish tucked under her skinny arm.

"Like cats and dogs, Della, I swear. Wadn't even a cloud in the sky more than a minute ago. Where in Sam Hill did this hurry-cane come from?" Lula bounded onto my front porch like a puppy dog, and she sat the damp sack of fish on the small card table next to my rusted wrought iron chair where I spent most of my time.

"You'se soaked to the bone, Lula," I took the sopping newspaper from her hand and threw it to the wastebasket that I kept beside my chair. It was full of pea shells.

"Otis suppost to pick me up by five o'clock and it's nearly twenty after. He ain't good for a thing. I guess he reckon he leave me in that sweaty old fish market all night. You mind I use your phone and ring my mama's house? I reckon he curled up sleeping like a cat on her sofa bed."

"Go ahead, Lula. Mind your voice, though. I got two babies in the back room sleepin', and Harlan is working the graveyard shift tonight. He's been trying to sleep since noon now. Lord knows you don't want to wake him. You ain't ever seen a man so angry as my Harlan when he sleep deprived."

"All right," Lula nodded as she opened the screen door and disappeared into the house.

I watched cars come and go from the fish market across Depot Street. Old colored men, and white men, alike, stood inside the building and peered out the large plate glass windows, watching the rain fall in sheets, waiting on just the right time to run to their cars parked in front of the old, white, cracked concrete building.

Women stood at the same kind of windows at the coin-op laundry mat next door to the market, holding their baskets of fresh folded laundry, waitin' on the same thing and wishin' the rain would stop for a moment so they could make a mad dash to their car and take their clean clothes home.

I was dry as a bone on the porch. Harlan had done a patch job on it the spring before and the only place it leaked was at the far end away from me. Water streamed through one small hole and emptied into a rusty tin bucket that I kept beneath it. I'd dump it in a larger bucket out back when the rain stopped. Then I'd use all that catch to give to my tomato plants in June when the Earth was dry as a bone and we wished for such a rain as this.

"He's there all right, sleeping like a kitten. You should'a heard my 84-year-old mama, bless her soul, yelling at Otis like he was a dog that done peed on her rug 'cause he left me down here so long. She swears he ain't good for nothing, and I got to agree with her. He sure ain't a thing like my older brother, Grover. Ain't one iota like Grover. Not one," Lula mumbled as she walked onto the porch and watched the rain slamming onto the railroad track next to the house. "You mind I sit with you a spell? Otis said he be here soon."

"Sit on, Lula. Mind the arm on that chair," I nodded at the dusty and navy blue wing back chair that sat in my mama's main room nearly fifty years before.

"Like sheets, ain't it?" Lula pulled her shawl around her dark, damp shoulders.

"It's springtime, all right, but I don't think I ever seen such a rain as this year. Harlan said the underpass was flooded the other night. He couldn't even get out to check on his folks on the west side of town. Said the Hatchie River is floodin' all the back roads. The soybean fields out on the west side look just like the bottom. I don't think I ever seen such rain as this," I thought out loud and grabbed the pouch of tobacco from my red apron pocket.

"Now, Della, don't tell me you still going about eating that man chew? How many teeth you done lost to that already? Been doin' that all your life, ain't ya? I bet you come out your mama with a pouch of tobacca," Lula laughed.

"I didn't do no such, Lula Perkins, but I wish I had. I ain't got a purpose for my own teeth anyhow. That doctor Milner popped me in some brand new teeth, and now I ain't got to worry about that," I smiled and showed Lula my bright white and straight teeth.

"I'll be," Lula shook her head as thunder rumbled in the distance. "My daddy chewed that kind of tobacca. You the only woman I ever saw that had a taste for it."

"Snuff'll do your heart good. Those young'uns get to screamin' in there? Harlan get to moaning about the chicken is burnt black? All I got to do is sit on my porch in my iron chair and chew my snuff, watch the rain, watch the train and all is right in my world," I spit the dark juice on the newspaper in the wastebasket.

"Della May, you a mess," Lula laughed and watched a white lady run from the laundry mat with her basket of linens. She fiddled with her keys; all the while the clean clothes in the wicker basket became soaked with rain.

"She in a pickle, that one," I said. "Shame she spent all that change to dry those clothes only to have 'em soaking wet again."

"Oh, Della! Did you hear about that girl over on Washburn Street? The jeweler's girl? The young'un?" Lula turned to me as my mama's old rickety chair creaked, her mouth dropped open.

"I ain't heard. What she do?" I asked.

"She's gone and vanished," Lula shrugged her shoulders. "She was supposed to come home from her daddy store yesterday but she just gone and vanished. Never came home."

"Say what? Washburn Street ain't a hop and a jump from her daddy's store. How she just vanish?" I ruffled my brow as brown juice dripped down my chin. I took my tattered apron and wiped it away.

"They thinkin' somebody snatched her up. Somebody had to have snatched her up. Otis told me he saw the police parked out front they house last night when he was comin' home from the pool hall. Said he saw her mama, that Mrs. Laney, pacing on the front porch. Said he could see the tears on that white lady's face as he drove by. Said her tears were big as quarters," Lula shook her head. "That's what Otis told me."

"I declare," I looked to the tan stockings covering my swollen feet. "I sure do hate to hear that. Mrs. Laney is an awfully good lady. Mr. Hill is good folks, too. They ain't never said a cross word about nobody that I know of. They always wavin' over here at me when they pick up fish plates on Thursday nights. They is good people as far as I know. That Mrs. Laney always got a smile."

"They older girl is around my Sonny's age. He heard down at the hardware store, straight from Mr. Downey's mouth, that she went off and married some Cajun man down in Naw'lins. Say she left home a few years ago and she ain't even been back. Say it broke that Mrs. Laney's heart in all kinds a' pieces. Now she done lost her other girl, too. I say a prayer for her last night. I reckon I say one tonight, too."

"Lord, I will, too. Bless her soul. Who would take that young'un like that? Ain't nothing bad like that happened in Hatchie County that I can ever remember. Surely we ain't got a kidnapper running around here? Why, I let my little Dorothy play out here on those tracks after dark last night. Somebody coulda got my baby girl, too. What's happened to this world, Lula? Ain't the same place where we growed up, that's for sure," I watched my small front yard turn into one large puddle.

"You keep an eye on the paper tomorrow. I bet they be a story in there about it. Otis said Mrs. Laney had tears the size of quarters," Lula picked at pink specks of faded polish on her yellow fingernails.

"I reckon I might go over there and pay Mrs. Laney a visit in a few days," the rain began to slacken. "Might take her a cobbler or offer to pray with her. I just ain't gonna imagine what she's feelin' about all this. I sure hate to hear it, Lula. Hatchie County is always been a safe place. We ain't ever had no one just vanish before."

"No young white ladies, at least. I know that colored boy out by the gin vanished when I's just a girl, but that didn't raise no eyebrows. It didn't make the paper, that's for sure, but we ain't ever had no white girls gone missing around here," Lula reached her hand over the side of the porch to feel the rain, "Rain bout to quit. Just a sprinkle now."

"I'm wonderin' if it ain't got nothing to do with her daddy being the jewel man. Those girls, Mrs. Laney too, always wearing some jewels. I'm wonderin' if somebody didn't take her just for a chain around her neck or a diamond in her ear lobes. Why else somebody take that girl?"

"Maybe she run off on her own, Della May. Maybe she had plenty of Hatchie County, Tennessee. She coulda had a car waitin' for her somewhere around Church Street. There's several alleyways over there. She coulda had a bag packed and a car waitin'. Why, she could be safe and sound in New York City right now with some big-timin' man!" Lula exclaimed as if she'd figured the whole thing out.

"That's nonsense, Lula," I spit the last bit of juice from my mouth and then chucked the worn tobacco in the wastebasket.

"Ain't all nonsense. Could be," Lula shrugged as if her feelings were hurt.

"You go on down to the police station and tell them just that, Lula Perkins. You a regular Sherlock Holmes," I grinned and tucked my hands deep into the pockets of my apron.

"There's Otis," Lula nodded to the old fifties model Plymouth Fury as it stopped out front of my house.

"Don't forget your fish," I nodded to the sack on the card table. "See you."

"Bye, now," she grabbed the paper sack and then stomped right through the puddle in the yard, her white canvas tennis shoes turning brown. She got in the car with Otis, and I saw her gums just flappin' as she yelled at him for being late.

The rain had completely stopped when Dorothy came onto the front porch, sleep in her eyes.

"When we eatin' supper, Granmaw?" she yawned and pulled a stray piece of hair tightly against her head.

"I'm goin' in to start supper. You stayin' out here?" I stood and straightened my aching back.

"Yessum," she walked down the porch steps and headed for the train track.

"Stay off them tracks, Dorothy. Stay up here on the porch where I can see ya," I said.

LEON, 1967

I placed the nails in a brown paper sack for Mr. Jensen as he laughed heartily with Daddy about his youngest boy trying to flush four toy trains down the toilet that morning.

"If I couldn't have gotten those things out of there, Billy, I'd been running down here for a plunger with my pants clear down 'round my ankles! After my coffee and cigarette, there are just some things I've got to do, if you get my drift?"

"I get you, Jensen. Lord, that would've been a sight, wouldn't it?" Daddy slapped him on the back as they walked toward the door. They cackled again as he exited and Daddy went to the back to finish inventory.

Mr. Jensen disappeared into his red Ford Galaxie parked in front of the store and I noticed her jogging across Main Street in an airy sundress with a teal ribbon flapping in her hair. I sprinted from behind the counter and hurried to the window so I could watch her walk to her daddy's store, but when she reached the sidewalk, she didn't turn left. She turned right. She turned right toward our hardware store.

I clumsily backed away from the window and checked my reflection in the nearest saw hanging from a hook. I licked the palm of my hand and tried to tame the obnoxious cowlick at the front of my forehead.

The bell on the door jingled, and she tucked the damp, sweaty strands of hair that had fallen loose from her ponytail behind her ears.

"Hey, Leon," she said without looking at me.

"Hey, Ellen," I swallowed the knot in my throat.

She sighed loudly and welcomed the air conditioning as she confidently walked to the back of the store. She seemed to know exactly what she needed.

"Can I- can I help you find something?" my voice cracked.

"I need to fix my suitcase," she mumbled as she reached for a roll of duct tape on the shelf.

"What's the problem, with, um, with your luggage?" I slowly approached her.

"The zipper is busted. I'm going to have to tape the thing closed," she examined the thick gray adhesive.

"Can't Mrs. Laney repair the zipper?" I could smell her now, sweat mixed with flowery perfume.

"I don't have time for that," she handed me the tape, still without looking at me, and then she walked to the counter.

I quickly followed behind her and stopped at the register.

"Going on a trip?" I asked.

"Yep," she nodded and pulled quarters from the small white change purse tucked in her hand.

"Where you headed?" I placed the tape in the paper sack and slid it across the counter.

"My boyfriend and I are going to New Orleans. I won't be back," she dropped the change in my hand, careful not to actually touch me. She grabbed the sack and headed for the door.

"You're leaving?" I blurted before realizing it.

She stopped and turned toward me, finally looking at me for the first time since she'd entered the store only a minute before, and my heart began to race. Just knowing her blue eyes were on me made me dizzy.

"That's right, Leon. That's devastating news to you, isn't it?" an arrogant grin covered her beautiful and fresh face.

"I-" I stammered and fidgeted with my hands concealed behind the counter, "I didn't even know you had a boyfriend. Anyone I might know?"

"I met him at a dance in Memphis this summer. He's a fisherman down in New Orleans. He'll he here by nightfall to take me back with him," she smirked.

I didn't know what to say. I was sure my mouth was dropped open, that depression was evident in my eyes, that my fidgeting was noticeable, even though my hands were still hidden behind the bulky counter.

"Good luck, Leon," her sneer softened into a genuine smile for a moment, and then she left the store. The sound of the door's bell resonated in my ears as I watched her jog across Main Street again, the paper sack hanging from her hand.

I'd watched Ellen Cooper walk down the hallway at school and bat her eyes at John William Brown for the last three years. Two years ago, when JW worked with us for the summer, I watched Charlotte Whitman march into the store and lean her voluptuous body across the counter. She tapped a hammer against her palm as she doted on Ellen and asked John William to give her a chance. I noticed Ellen scurry by the store three times while Charlotte was putting in a good word for her.

When Charlotte left, I asked John William why he didn't appreciate such a pretty girl's efforts, but he said he was all hung up on that white trash Willard girl out on Route 8. Sometimes I wanted to shake some sense into him. I wanted to shake him for being too damn stupid to see what he was missing with Ellen Cooper. Other times I was so jealous that Ellen loved him instead of me that I wanted to bash in his head with the very hammer that Charlotte had held in her hand.

When John William moved down to Mississippi last summer, I thought that maybe I'd finally get a chance to call on Ellen. Barry Warren had the same idea. So did Jack Christian and a few other boys around town, but Ellen was in some sort of mourning since John William had gone.

She missed a lot of school when he moved down to Itta Bena. She didn't care about cheerleading or senior prom or even her grades. Mrs. Morrison scolded her in front of the whole Algebra class because her A+ average had dropped to a D. She only replied with some snide remark and stormed out of the classroom.

She stayed shut up in her house on Washburn Street, and for some God-forsaken reason, she started palling around with the Darnell twins that lived in the old slave house behind her daddy's property. Those girls were quite a few years older than we were and they took a lot of trips down to Memphis for the weekend. Rumor had it that they hung around the blues bars and drank whiskey with musicians all night. I knew Ellen's mama and daddy fretted over her hanging around with those sisters. I'd heard Mr. Hill Cooper stand right at the front of our store and tell Daddy that he didn't know what in the world to do with Ellen. He said teenage girls were the most confusing species on the planet. Daddy didn't have any girls, but he agreed.

I was hoping that Ellen would snap out of it. I was hoping that she'd get over that ignorant JW Brown now that he wasn't even in Tennessee anymore, that she'd realize that there was more to life than him and that she'd just snap out of it. I was hoping that she'd quit associating with those wild and crazy Darnell girls and that she'd return to her proper place in the upper-crust social circle with Charlotte Whitman and Susan Ansley, but it didn't look like she was going to snap out of it at all. Now she was running off to New Orleans with some unknown Cajun fisherman, and I knew I'd probably never see her again.

John William Brown had ruined her life.

And he'd ruined mine.

MRS. COLBY, 1972

Janette hadn't been gone from the jewelry store for five minutes and I was already going behind her to do the work that she'd failed to do. She'd left dust an inch thick on the wedding china and fingerprints covered the glass case that held the watches. I didn't understand why she'd done such a poor job today. That girl was usually on point when she helped around the store. She was usually on point with everything.

I'd been working in this jewelry store on Main Street since Hill purchased it from Mr. Hartsfield in 1953. Hill's mother, Sue Ellen Cooper, and I had been the best of friends all of our lives. We grew up together out on Cherryville Chapel Road and boy did we make some fine memories. It was some kind of terrible hurt to me when she passed away a few days before Hill purchased the building. She was awful excited about her only son's new business and she had planned to help him run the place. When she suddenly died, I gladly offered to do the job.

I loved Hill Cooper like he was my own son. I'd watched him grow up and turn into a fine Christian man. I loved his wife, Laney, like a daughter and his girls, Ellen and Janette, like my own grandchildren. My husband, Herbert, and I never had any children of our own, so Sue Ellen's family was a real blessing to me. I wouldn't trade them for nothing.

When Hill's eldest daughter, Ellen, ran off with some Cajun drunkard five years ago, we all ached at the loss. We didn't know where she'd taken a wrong turn, but she'd taken it all right. She rarely called her mama or daddy now days and the hurt at her absence was always apparent in Hill's tired eyes. He often talked about driving down to Naw'lins to get her and bring her back home, but he never did it. I think he really wanted to go get his little girl, but Laney just wouldn't let him go. I'd heard her say so many times, "If she doesn't want to come home, well, we can't make her." I guess that was true.

I'd lived in Hatchie County my whole life so I knew everyone that set foot in the store. Helping my longtime friend's grandchildren pick out wedding bands and getting the latest gossip from the customers was my purpose in my old age, and I didn't mind it one bit. I'd always liked fine jewelry and gossip anyway.

As I dusted shelves or polished rings, I'd gaze out the storefront windows overlooking Main Street and examine the townsfolk. I watched Mr. Hunter sneak out the back door of the Commerce and Trust to smoke a cigarette every afternoon before he headed home to his nagging wife who forbade tobacco. I watched the patrons at the hardware store lug newly-purchased tools out to their cars and trucks, with a look of determination to finish projects on their faces. Sometimes Marvin would bring me a hot plate lunch from his diner and we'd talk about his wife's crippling arthritis. Old Henry McMillan would stop in just to explain what exactly quartz was to me and I'd wonder if he was quite right in the head. It was a small town, but I knew everyone in it. I guess that made me feel sort of proud.

"Janette didn't figure the books correctly today," Hill mumbled as he walked out of his office at the back of the store, a cloud of cigar smoke trailing him. "That girl has always been good with figures."

"She didn't dust these shelves worth a darn, either. What's going on in that girl's head today?" I raked the feathers across the glass cases and sent the dust into the air to mingle with the stench of Hill's Cubans.

"I don't know what goes on in the mind of young girls, Mrs. Colby. You know that," he sat down at the main jewelry case to examine the new inventory.

"No word from Ellen lately?" I inquired as I checked my reflection in the glass cabinet. I licked a smudge of lipstick from my teeth and noticed the sad state of my dyed hair. My 72-year-old locks had lost all of their natural curl. It was time for another permanent.

"She called us a few nights ago. She was so drunk I couldn't even make out what she was saying. All I heard were trombones and slurs," he shook his head in disappointment.

"I'm awful sorry, Hill, but she'll find her way back. I know it in my heart of hearts. That girl will be back."

"I'm not so sure," Hill sighed and pulled a sapphire from the case. "She's been gone five years now, so I'm not so sure."

"Sometimes young ladies need a while to figure things out, Hill. Don't fret on it, son," I said.

I knew Ellen probably wouldn't come back to Hatchie County. She'd taken up with liquor and the New Orleans lifestyle. She was hooked on all of that voodoo and other nonsense down there and it was bound to keep her hooked and then kill her. I hated to think such a thought, but we all knew it was true. It was such a shame, too, because she'd always been such a nice girl. She'd just taken a wrong turn and she'd taken it hard.

"How's Mr. Herbert feeling today?" Hill changed the subject.

"Well," I put the feather duster behind the counter, "all this rain has kept him inside, you know. He sure was glad to see a break in it today. Said he'd try to do some work on the barn."

"I don't like all of the work he does around your place; climbing ladders and such. At his age, it just isn't safe. Why don't you tell him to wait on whatever chores he has and I'll be glad to help him in a few days. Forecast said the rain will be back tonight, but it ought to clear off by the weekend."

"Well, I try, Hill," I argued. "I've told him that countless times, but you know my Herbert. He's stubborn as that old mule out in our pasture. I can't peg him down for a minute. Never could."

Hill laughed, "Well, you're right about that."

"That Stanley Willard came by last week begging to do some odd jobs around the place. Herbert wouldn't let him lift a finger. I told Herbert that work would be good for that old boy, but he just gave him a few bucks and sent him on his way. He just gave him that money without lifting a finger for it! You know Stanley drank it all up, but Herbert wouldn't listen to me. He's stubborn as a mule, like I said."

"I wouldn't trust Stanley Willard to work on my barn either," Hill placed the loupe on his glasses and examined another ring.

"Well you might be right about that," I looked around the store to make sure I'd destroyed all of the dust. "You know I heard Stanley's daughter moved down to Itta Bena to be with that John William Brown. They've got her moved right into the Brown house. I don't know how in the world John William ever talked his mama into that one. I remember Lil putting up quite the fuss about her boy running around with that Willard girl and now she's moved right in her house. I wonder what changed."

"I don't have a clue, Mrs. Colby," Hill said, uninterested.

"You know Ellen had a mighty strong feeling about that John William at one time. She rushed around town in white dresses in the middle of cotton-pickin' season just hoping to catch a glimpse of that boy at Downey's store. Those dresses would turn dark as mud from all the dust floating around but she didn't care. That's what love does, I guess. He was always a good boy, too, that John William. I wish that had worked out." I thought aloud.

"Well," he sighed, "I do, too. I'd rather have her down in Itta Bena in Lil Brown's house than in that Bordeaux fella's shack in Naw'lins doing God knows what."

"I know you would," I patted his shoulder and realized I never should have said anything.

"This one would look nice soldered with a diamond band," Hill continued to inspect the ring.

I leaned over his shoulder to see the sparkling jewel. “Yes, it would.”

The phone rang and I walked back to Hill’s office to answer it. I removed the pearl bob from my ear, placed it on his desk and picked up the receiver.

“Cooper’s Jewelry Store,” I answered. “Why no, Laney. Janette left here nearly 20 minutes ago.”

JOHN WILLIAM BROWN, 1978

There wasn't any place more peaceful on God's great earth than my mama's front porch. After a long day at the firm, I'd often drive out to her place on the north side of town just to sit in her scuffed white rocking chair, drink a cold one and watch the deer move at dusk. There was a 12-point beast that hung around only 150 yards or so from her house, but I couldn't bring myself to shoot him. I liked watching him grunt proudly at his devoted doe too much to mount his rack on my office wall.

Mama was quite lonely now that daddy was buried beneath the Weeping Willow past the duck pond. She tried to keep busy baking and volunteering and playing Rook with her friends, but the void his death left was great. Her face lit up every time she saw me walking up the creaky painted steps of the porch. I'd loosen my tie and she'd rush out to bring me a cold glass bottle of Budweiser that she kept stocked in her refrigerator just for me.

Sometimes Mama would sit with me on the porch and we'd talk. We talked about Daddy and how the hired hands didn't take care of the place with the efficiency or passion that he had. Now days we often talked about my old lady, too. Just saying her name in an uncondescending tone was a new thing for Mama, but my wife was pregnant with her first grandchild, so that made the difference. Mama didn't love the mother of my future child- she never had loved Caroline and probably never would- but she already loved her grandbaby.

Sometimes she'd let me sit on the porch alone, with my thoughts and my glass bottle, because she knew I needed silence. Mama was the only woman who could read me. She'd pop onto the porch to trade my empty bottle for a full one, and then she'd leave me to the songs of the crickets while the sun set.

While watching the sky turn from hues of pink and orange to finally black, I usually thought about my wife and the little girl who would be here any day now. I was nervous about becoming a father. That's why I started drinking after work every day, just to help me calm down a little bit about the change that was soon to come. I promised my wife I'd stop the binging as soon as the baby was born, but I wasn't sure if she believed me. I didn't see the harm in having a couple of beers after a hard day of work, but my wife loathed alcohol and never wanted to settle down with a drinking man.

I also drank because my 30th birthday was quickly approaching. I didn't know where the time had gone or when I'd become old enough to be a lawyer, a husband and a father. It seemed just like yesterday I was playing sandlot baseball on the corner of Herndon and Hooper in Hatchie County. Boy, those were some carefree days.

I had a wonderful childhood in Tennessee, and I was a pretty popular kid. All the guys wanted to throw a curveball like me and all the gals wanted to watch me throw the curveballs. I'd say life was pretty good in Hatchie County in the 1960's. Leon, David, Hartley and I started a band, "Four on the Floor", and we won two pretty big talent shows in Memphis with our cover of "A Hard Day's Night". We strutted down the school halls like celebrities for months. Hartley even referred to himself as "McCartney" for a while.

Sure, I also made some bad decisions back then, but what teenage boy didn't? I once climbed aboard a stopped train on Depot Street, thinking I'd just jump off at the crossing nearby my house. I don't know how cowboys do it in old westerns because those things pick up a lot of speed. I just couldn't bring myself to jump and risk messing up the arm that was responsible for all of those curveballs. So I had no choice but to use my belt to strap onto the ladder of a boxcar and ride it all the way to Memphis. I was frozen stiff by the time the train finally stopped down by the Mississippi River and I had to find some way to warm up. It only made sense for me to go into a laundry mat and use a dryer to warm my hands. Only thing is, after I dumped a ton of change into the machine, it would cut off every time I opened the door to put my hands inside.

Freezing to the bone was nothing compared to the ride back home with my daddy, John Senior, that night. I've never been as scared as I was on that two hour ride back from Memphis. I tried to laugh about it with Dad years after it happened, but he never thought it was funny. I guess he died thinking that was one of the dumbest damn things I ever did.

Of course Mama would say one of the dumbest damn things I ever did was marry my wife. She never thought she was good enough to carry our last name, and she outlawed our relationship from the get-go. She claimed moving us from Hatchie County, Tennessee down to Itta Bena, Mississippi after I graduated high school was so we could take care of her spinster sister, Beck, but I know she was really determined to get me away from "that white trash Willard girl".

I could've had my pick of many girls- rich ones, classy ones, gorgeous ones- but none of them compared to my brown-eyed beauty. Even after our move to Mississippi, she and I still stayed in contact. I told Mama that I wanted her to move down here from Tennessee because she was in such a bad environment back home with her drunkard daddy, but Mama refused. I sent for her anyway and told Mama if she didn't let her stay in the guest house on the very land where that monster 12-point now roamed that I was going to drop out of college, marry her and run off to Biloxi or somewhere. Mama reluctantly agreed.

Mama would hardly mumble two words to Caroline, even though she walked over from the guest house every morning and gladly helped care for Aunt Beck right up until she died. She also cooked and cleaned and earned her keep and treated Mama with respect she sometimes didn't deserve. It was a lot of tension in the house, and we finally married once I finished law school, but Mama didn't even show up to the wedding. Daddy was there, though, and he even offered to give my bride away. Daddy knew that although my love didn't come from very good parents, she was a kind girl and he knew she'd make a good wife. Daddy could see that she certainly loved me more than life itself and that's what mattered.

I knew that sweet, brown-eyed wife of mine didn't deserve a husband who snuck off to his mother's house for a few beers every afternoon. She'd grown up with a drunk and had never planned on marrying one. But I really was going to stop once the baby got here. I was just so overwhelmed and maybe a little depressed, too, with getting older and becoming a father. The tension between her and my Mama and not having Daddy around as a buffer made it all right for me to have a couple of drinks, right? I really was going to stop once the baby got here.

"John William," Mama quickly swung the screen door open and bounded onto the porch. "Cora Lee just called! Caroline is having the baby!"

My mama's announcement gave birth to a million different emotions, so I guzzled the rest of my beer, jumped into Mama's Impala and we headed to the hospital to meet my baby girl.

LILLIAN ODIE BROWN, 1993

I've seen a lot of unfair things in my 70 years. I've seen a lot of things that just didn't seem right or good happen to right and good people. I've questioned my faith and my God about those things, but I never did seem to get a real answer. I guess my answer will come when I'm finally face to face with my Maker, which I hope is sooner than later.

I've watched my baby brother, Hassell, hobble around on one leg for most of his life. I've watched him fasten shiny pins to an empty trouser leg, grip a battered cane with weak hands and gaze in jealousy as my son rounded the bases, wishing he could still do the same. I watched a young and swift man leave for the war and return an old cripple. That never seemed fair to me.

I watched my older sister, Beck, live a long, lonely life in a dilapidated farmhouse on a cool hill. I'd seen her pull her coat close to her body when the autumn wind blew, wishing instead it were a man to warm her in his arms. I watched my spinster sister wilt away and be put to rest with no husband or children to weep over her grave. That never seemed fair to me.

I left my childhood home and my parents in Itta Bena to make a life with my new husband in Hatchie County. I enjoyed most of my time in Hatchie County, but the years spent away from my true home of Mississippi made me resentful in so many ways. That never seemed fair to me.

I let my smoky old boss at the bank, Mr. Hunter, whisper vile things into my ear and put his arms around my waist, leaving me uncomfortable and violated. Nearly every day I wanted to quit that job, but I couldn't because I had to help put food on our table. That never seemed fair to me.

I watched a young boy named Henry McMillin walk around with a head full of knowledge that could have taken him anywhere in this world, but he couldn't even tie his own shoelaces, so he was destined to live his life with his mother. That never seemed fair to me.

I received letters from my good friend, Laney Cooper, who had lost her oldest daughter to rebellion and alcohol and Louisiana voodoo. She wrote to me about the shame that she felt and the eyes that took pity upon her when she walked to her husband's jewelry store. Once her heart was nearly broken in two at that loss, her baby girl, her reason for living, suddenly and mysteriously vanished. I went up to visit her in Hatchie County, only to find a woman with dead eyes- empty eyes and an empty soul- a woman who had lost more than she could bear. That never seemed fair to me.

I read in the Hatchie County paper about young, awkward Leon Downey, who left his inherited hardware store behind to go searching for that troubled girl in New Orleans, only to be robbed and killed on a street corner. That never seemed fair to me.

I heard a tragic tale about the sweetest colored lady I ever knew in Hatchie County, Della May. She took care of children and grandchildren her entire life, but the moment the cancer was discovered, her children stuck her in a home to be eaten up and die alone. That never seemed fair to me.

I watched Stanley Willard's no-good, white-trash daughter hang onto my only son's every word and cast glaring eyes my way just to remind me that she'd won. She'd somehow conned him into loving her, despite my pleas that he stay away from her. She'd weaseled into our Mississippi home. She'd wriggled right into a wedding band. She'd won my boy- my boy who deserved so much better in this life. That never seemed fair to me.

I've seen some awful unfair things in my life, but the worst of all is that my sister-in-law, who has been dying since the day she was born, outlived my only child.

Now I've got the same look as Laney Cooper. I'm about as hollow as the dead hickory on my property line. I feel like the most important thing in my life is missing, just like my baby brother felt about his leg that was left in an Okinawan ditch.

Caroline keeps saying my John William's death should bring the two of us closer together, but I'd rather rest next to my husband and my son under that Weeping Willow tree past the duck pond than ever form a bond with her. I'd just rather shrivel up and die than cast a smile her way or take her into an embrace. Besides, it's probably her fault that my son drank himself to death. All her nagging and complaining and spending his hard-earned money on her fancy dresses is what made him reach for the bottle and ruin his liver. I just know it.

The only good thing Caroline ever did for me was give me a granddaughter. I couldn't love that little girl more. I cherish the summers we've spent together, the talks and the games of Rook. I can't help but gleam when I look at her, either. She's got my John William's eyes, smile and mannerisms. She's a Brown, through and through. I don't see a speck of Willard in that girl.

Cora Lee Helpless, with her malignant this and throbbing that and her imminent death that's lasted over 60 years, is sitting next to my baby brother with the shiny pin and the knotted cane in a retirement home on Main Street. They watch the cars go by as they fan themselves with newspapers and yell over the creaking of rockers. Cora Lee declares to Hassell that it's probably her last day on earth, all the while my young boy, only 44-years-old, turns to dust. That will never seem fair to me.

I've seen some unfair things in my lifetime, but I don't know how I'll ever cope with that old invalid still breathing this fresh, Mississippi air all the while my boy does not. I feel dead and numb to the world and everyone in it, but that precious granddaughter of mine is the only thing that keeps me going.

Thank God she doesn't look like her mama- that drunken horse man's daughter- that white trash Willard girl.

JANETTE COOPER, 1972

Here I was travelling miles away from the only home I'd ever known; sailing down unknown highways, further and further away from my mother's peach cobblers and my father's boisterous hugs. Here I was leaving everything behind and it was all John William Brown's fault.

They must've been in hysterics by now. Daddy was probably out pacing Washburn Street and praying I'd top the hill and finally be in his sight. Mama was on the phone with every lady in town, praying for a clue. My friends were in a tizzy. Mrs. Colby asked her Herbert to fire up his old truck and comb all of the back roads. The police were probably there, too. Chief Gaskins was loosening his cheap, slim tie as he took notes.

She dusted the jewelry store around noon and then headed home. Kidnapping? Any drifters seen around town? Unfamiliar cars? Interview the hobos down by the fish market. Mysterious strangers? No stone left unturned.

It isn't very difficult to find a mysterious stranger to drive you out of state- to drive you out west where the air is dry and better on asthmatic lungs. All you have to do is find a scraggly-looking drifter hanging around at the depot- those drifters who never spend more than a day or two in Hatchie County eating leftover hushpuppies from the fish market and begging for odd jobs that have already been claimed by Stanley Willard. That scraggly-looking drifter knows a guy who makes people disappear. He'll send that guy to wait for you in an old Plymouth behind the record store. You'll hand him a wad of cash that you've saved- and stolen here or there- and then he'll crank that old Plymouth and leave town. We'll leave Hatchie County, together, in the spring drizzle and drive straight to Arizona- where the air is clear and no one knows my name.

I didn't want to leave. I had a wonderful childhood in my dusty southern town. I was blessed with good hard-working parents and loyal friends. I even thought I was destined to marry the youngest Whitman boy and eventually move down to Memphis where he'd work in a high-rise and I'd sip mint juleps on the patio and host classy parties for the review club. I'd get a new diamond for every occasion, a new car every two years, and all would be right in my world. That's how it was supposed to be.

But my sister sure mucked that up. She ruined my life, and her own, and it was all John William Brown's fault.

Ever since she was a young girl, she was obsessed with John William and her own dreams of mint juleps and fancy parties. She sat in her bed late at night, crying and praying that he'd choose her. He never chose her, though. For some godforsaken reason he chose Stanley Willard's daughter with her ratty dresses and tragic childhood and then he left Hatchie County. My sister was heartbroken, and not just the regular ole heartbroken. She was completely broken. She was so grieved that she lost her mind.

She went wild and spent most of her time in scandalous bars down in Memphis, associating with some Cajun no-good who kept her liquored up and introduced her to pills and pipes. She actually laughed when she told me the story of waking up in a motel room wearing nothing but pantyhose and clutching Mama's pearls. She fell in love with that life of destruction, and she, too, left Hatchie County- the only town she'd ever known.

"Good riddance," I thought when Mama read aloud the note Ellen had left behind. I mean, I loved my sister, and we were pretty close before John William left her broken. But I saw the pain she caused my parents, so when she left, I thought it was a blessing. But it turned out to be the worst thing to ever happen to me.

Once she was gone, Mama and Daddy both changed. They tightened their grip on me and I wasn't even allowed to leave the house. They feared I was going to go crazy like my sister, and it must have been a crime the way they kept me locked away from the world. I had to come home directly after school, and I wasn't allowed to go anywhere on the weekends but to church and my father's jewelry store. It baffled me, really, because I wasn't anything like my sister, Ellen. I'd never been hung up on a boy the way she was hung up on John William. I sure wasn't crying over the youngest Whitman every night or contemplating running down to voodoo country to get high and waste my life away. I was nothing like Ellen at all, but my parents were so scared that I would follow in her footsteps and take a wrong turn.

I had to sneak out of the house to meet my friends, to meet the drifter down at the depot. I'd return home, unharmed, and they'd shout and ground me for another month, another two months. They smothered me, through and through, and they had no signs of relenting.

I couldn't take it anymore. My parents said they weren't even going to let me go off to college. I was destined to work in my daddy's store for the rest of my life. They didn't want me to meet any boys, not even good respectable ones like the youngest Whitman. They aimed to keep me home for the rest of my life as an old spinster maid. And they aimed to do this, they claimed, out of love.

There was no way I was going to spend my life in Hatchie County, dusting jewelry cases with Mrs. Colby and rocking on my parent's front porch as all of my friends courted and went off to school. I cursed my sister, and I cursed John William Brown, as I made secret plans to leave on my own. There was no other way, no easier way, to regain my life but to run away. And running away is pretty easy to do if you have a fistful of dollars and a guy in a Plymouth waiting on you in an alley.

Damn that John William Brown. If my sister had never been hung up on him, this wouldn't have happened. If only he'd chosen her instead of Caroline Willard, then I'd still be eating my mama's peach cobblers, handing my daddy a pack of matches for his cigars and taking walks with young Whitman, as we planned our future and went house shopping in midtown Memphis.

Riding in that Plymouth to Arizona, with a scruffy guy with missing teeth and a scar over his left eyebrow, was all John William Brown's fault. That's where I'd always lay the blame.

No one knew where I was going. No one would find me. I'd live my life in Arizona with the desert air and the desert view. I'd start out waitressing or bookkeeping and then I'd meet just the right man. We'd marry and raise children there in that desert and I'd learn to forget my mama, my daddy, my drunkard sister and that damn John William Brown.

No one knew how I'd vanished except Henry McMillin. He watched me ride right down Washburn Street with the scruffy mysterious stranger in the Plymouth. I even gave him a little nod and a wave as thunder bellowed and I passed by my house for the last time.

But he wasn't telling nobody.

Made in the USA
Middletown, DE
12 April 2017